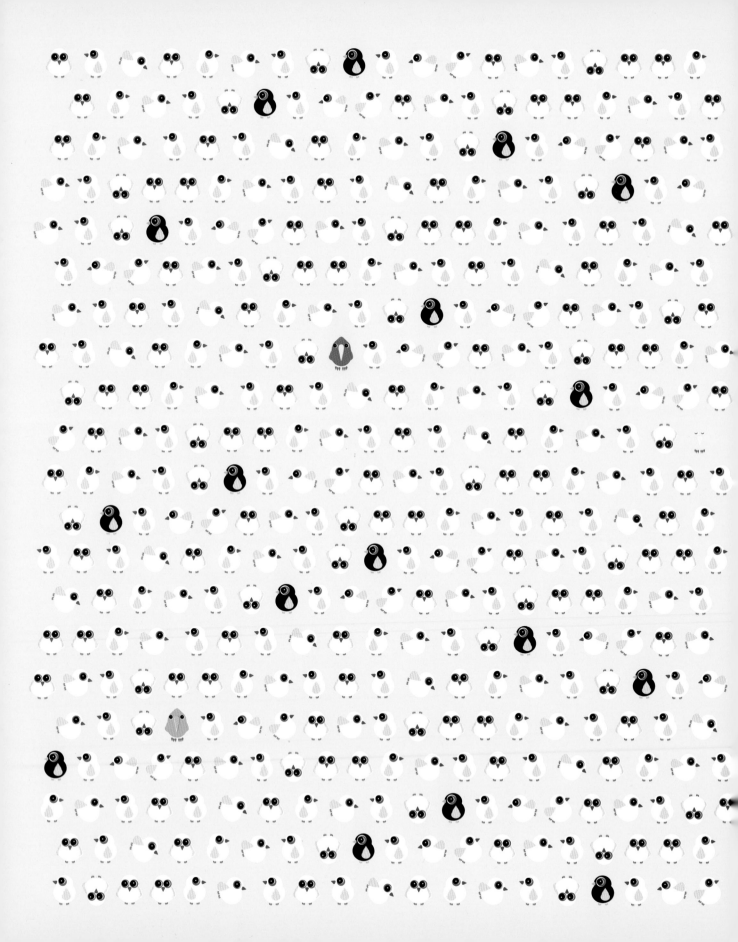

MOKO-MAKI!

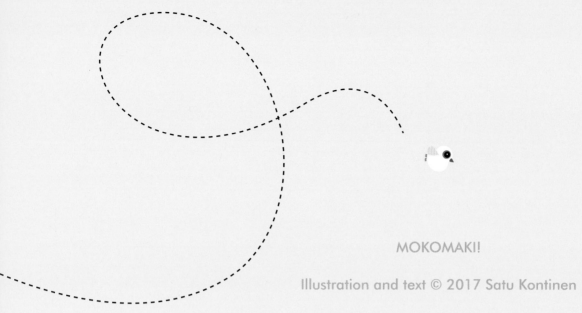

MOKOMAKI!

Illustration and text © 2017 Satu Kontinen

Published by POW!
a division of powerHouse Packaging & Supply, Inc.
- 32 Adams Street, Brooklyn, NY 11201-1021

info@powkidsbooks.com
www.powkidsbooks.com
www.powerHouseBooks.com
www.powerHousePackaging.com

Library of Congress Control Number: 2017943910

ISBN: 978-1-57687-805-7

10 9 8 7 6 5 4 3 2 1

Printed in Malaysia

MOKO-MAKI!

SATU KONTINEN

Why are you all upside down?

Let's investigate!

I'm gonna find her first.

Come on fellas, a little fox has gone missing!

POW!

BROOKLYN, NY

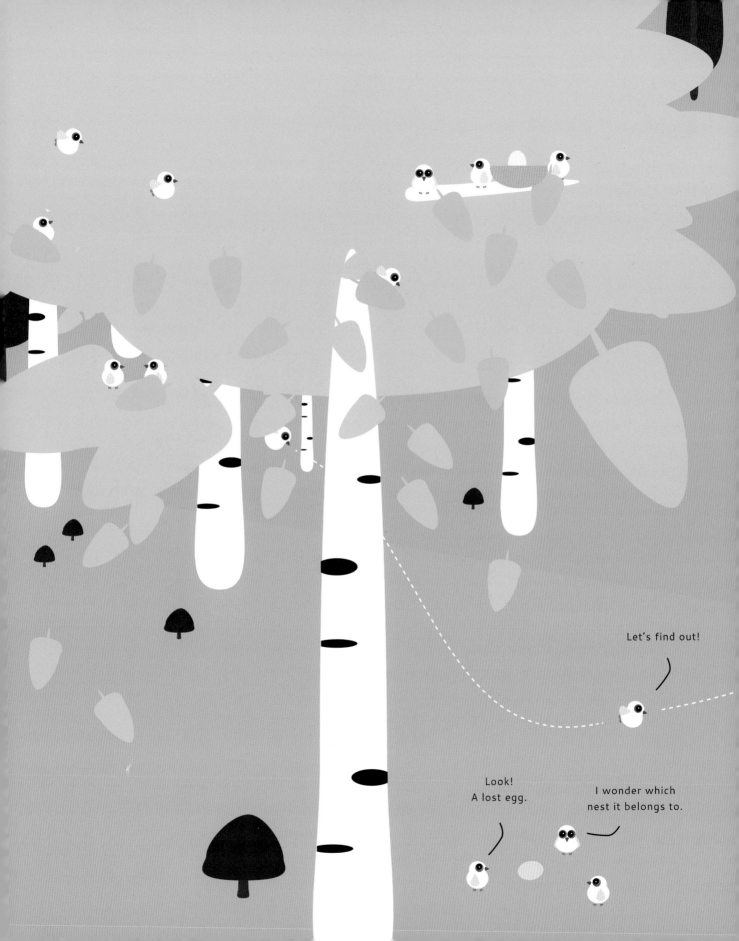

Let's find out!

Look!
A lost egg.

I wonder which
nest it belongs to.

HI, MOKOMAKI!
CAN YOU FIND MY LITTLE GIRAFFE?
HE'S THE TINIEST OF ALL.

What's
this about?

Let's help!
Which one is
the smallest?

Shall we
count them?

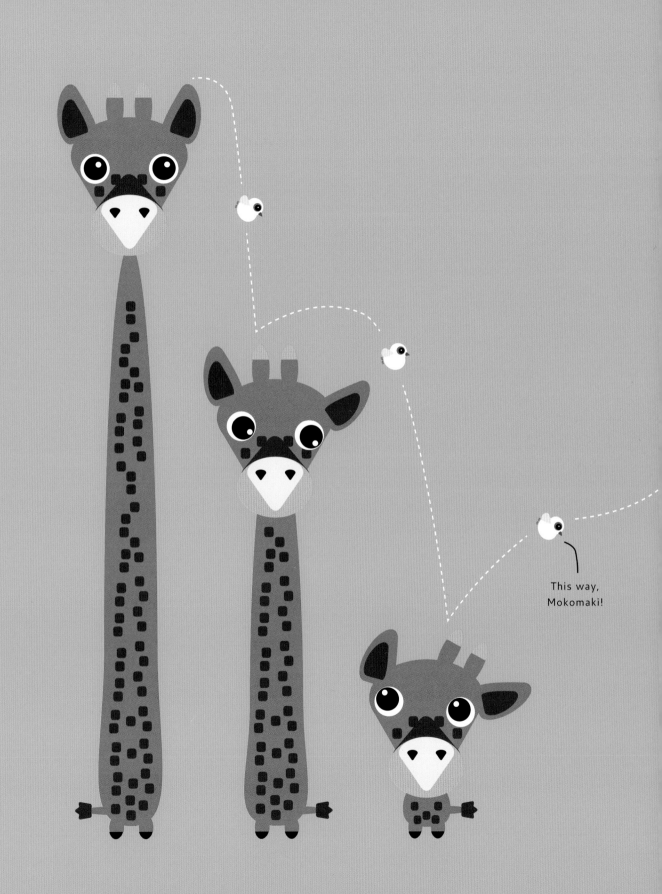

This way, Mokomaki!

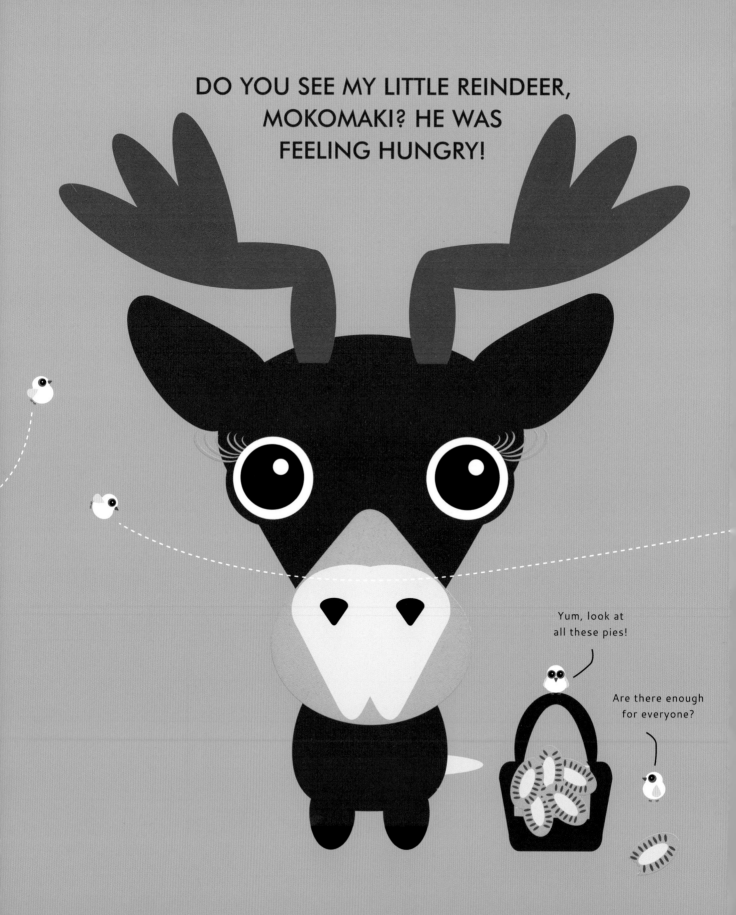

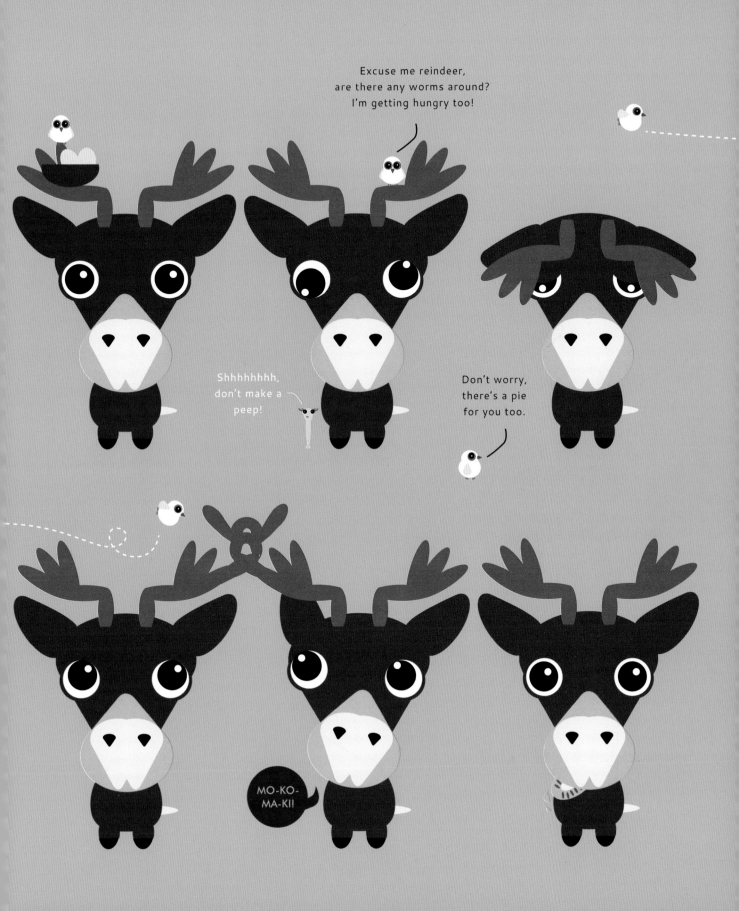

OH HELP ME, MOKOMAKI.
I CAN'T FIND MY LITTLE LION,
HE'S FALLEN FAST ASLEEP.

Are these
foxes?

Look at all
the different
whiskers!

Which lion
has the
longest?

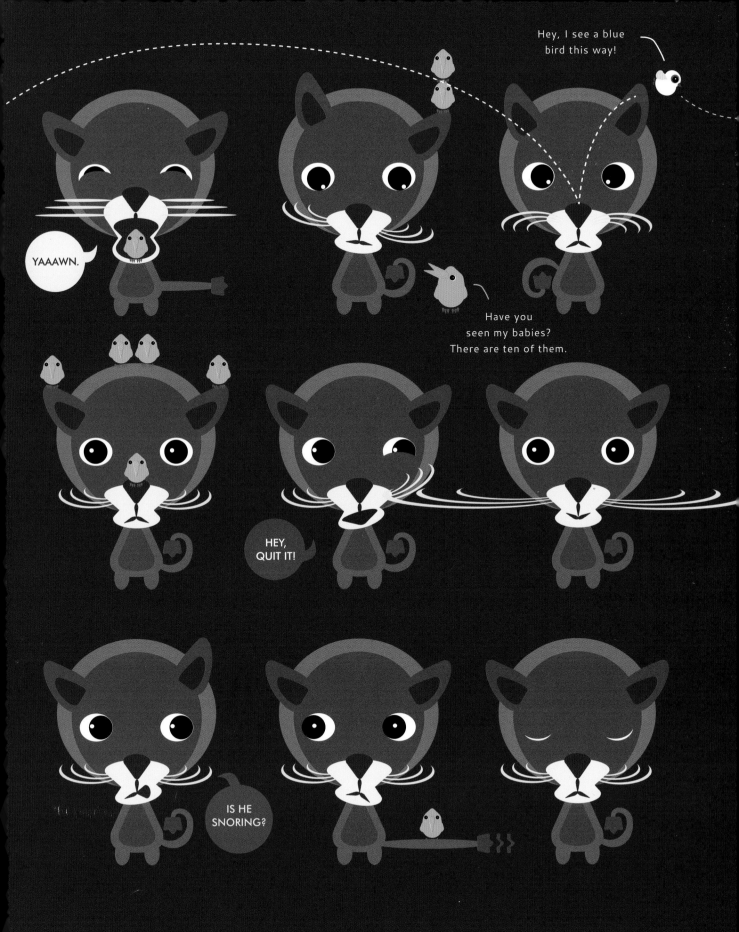

DEARIE ME! MOKOMAKI,
CAN YOU FIND MY LITTLE ZEBRA?
SHE LOST HER STRIPES!

THESE AREN'T MINE!

Have you seen my brothers? They look like me!

MOKOMAKI, CAN YOU FIND
MY LITTLE BLUE BIRD?
SHE REALLY BLENDS IN!

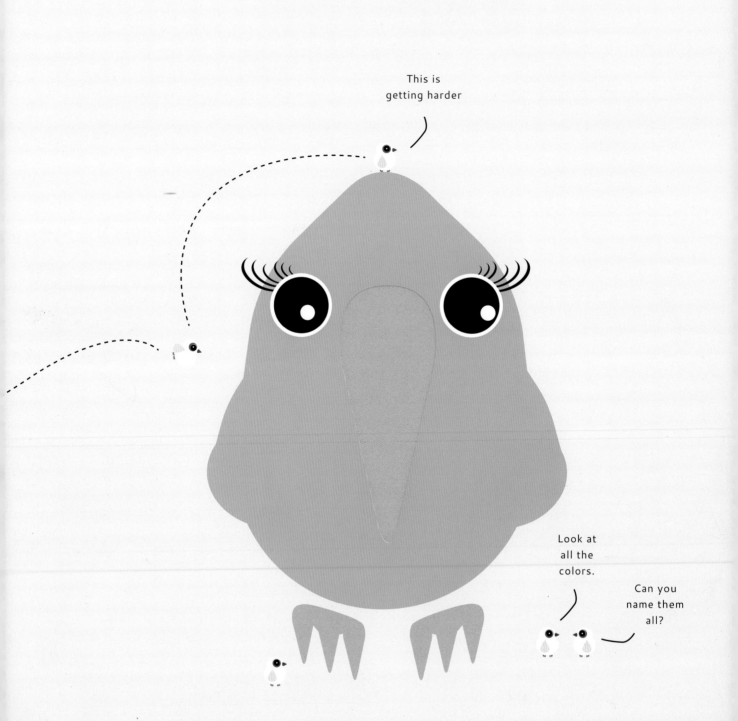

IT'S NOT ME.

Do I smell fish?

Eeek!

MY LITTLE MONKEY TWINS ARE MISSING, MOKOMAKI, DO YOU SEE THEM? THEY TIED THEIR TAILS IN KNOTS!

MY BABY BEAR IS SAFE WITH ME,
BUT LITTLE FOX IS STILL MISSING!
DON'T GIVE UP, MOKOMAKI!

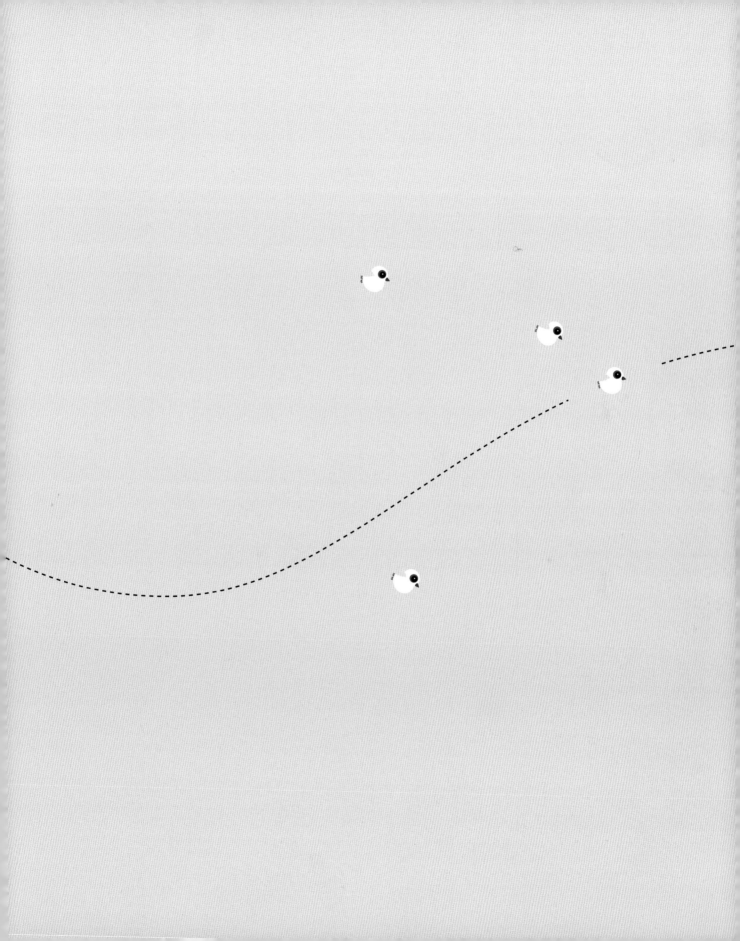

Mokomaki,
I think I see him!

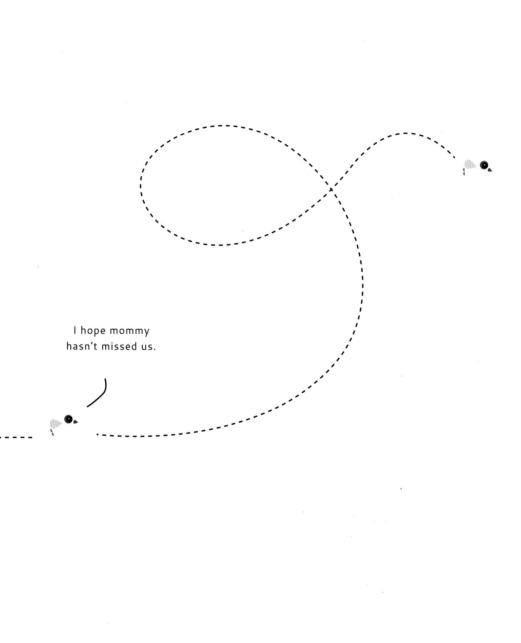